Gothenburg, the old Swedish port where Magnus lives, is a city with busy streets and even busier people — most of whom have little time and less patience to spare for a lonely seven year old. But luckily for Magnus, he has his grown-up friend Matthew to rely on — for talks and, better still, occasional rides on his motorcycle.

When Matthew's motorcycle turns up unexpectedly, without Matthew, Magnus summons all his courage (and an enormous Saint Bernard dog) to search the old harbor for his friend.

Magnus
in the Harbor

Magnus in the Harbor

by Hans Peterson

Translated by Marianne Turner

Drawings by Ilon Wikland

PANTHEON BOOKS

First American Edition
© Copyright, 1962, by Burke Publishing Company Ltd.
All rights reserved under International and Pan-American Copyright
Conventions. Published in New York by Pantheon Books, a division of
Random House, Inc. Originally published in Swedish as "Magnus I
Hamn" © Copyright, 1958, by Rabén & Sjögren.
Library of Congress catalog card number: AC 66-10358
Manufactured in the United States of America

Contents

Magnus
in the Harbor

1

The Heat Wave

IN a week's time they were going to move. Magnus looked gloomy as he sat finishing his breakfast.

"Cheer up!" called Mother. "You know we're all going to like it very much better in our new apartment."

"How do you know we are?" sighed Magnus.

"Because we're going to live in a brand new block, and there are three rooms in the apartment. You'll have a room all to yourself there, so you won't have to sleep in an alcove off the kitchen any more, and . . ."

"But I like it here," said Magnus.

The more he thought about it, the more he liked it. He

had slept in this kitchen for as long as he could remember, and that was quite a long time, because this summer he was eight. He liked this kitchen. He liked listening to the sounds coming from the waterpipes, the buzzing of solitary flies against the windowpane, and watching the sunbeams peep around the side of the blind when he woke in the morning — in the summer, that was. In the winter it was dark even when he went off to school. It was summer now, and the window was left open at night, and he could hear lots of sounds from outside as he settled down to sleep.

The block where Magnus lived was right in the center of Gothenburg, a big city in Sweden. From the courtyard, paved with cobblestones, there was an archway leading on to the narrow street which joined East Hamn Street to West Hamn Street. The two broad Hamn Streets were dense with traffic because it was the tourist season. People came to see the great harbor with its hundreds and hundreds of big ships which loaded and unloaded their cargos. They came to see the Shipping Museum and the vast Slotts Park.

Once Magnus had had a baby squirrel — his friend Matthew had given it to him. When Magnus couldn't keep it in the apartment any longer because it was growing too big, he and Matthew took it up to Slotts Park and let it loose there. Sometimes when Magnus went to Slotts Park with Matthew, he often thought it was his own squirrel that he saw, jumping from one great tree to another. But he was never quite certain — the worst part about squirrels is that they are all so very much alike.

The tourists also visit Liseberg which is a great amusement park with trees and lawns and waterfalls, roller coasters, helter-skelters, swings, merry-go-rounds, rifle-ranges and lots of other things besides. In the daytime they drive to the coast, or else they board the gleaming white steamers which take them to any one of the thousands of islands nearby from which they can swim. Gothenburg is on the sea, and the water is crystal clear and very salty. The streets are jammed with the tourists, cars driving side by side with the blue trams and buses, with trucks and with motorcycles, so that if you are on foot you feel you're walking in danger of your life. But Magnus had spent all his life within a stone's throw of the busy East Hamn Street, and he was used to the traffic. He always waited by the yellow lines at the pedestrian crossing until all the cars had stopped, then he marched across. It is not at all difficult once you know how and don't rush back-and-forth like small children.

At night Magnus could hear many different noises through the kitchen window, especially in the summer — laughing, shouting, the screeching of brakes, a fire engine rushing past, trams rattling . . . The night was full of sounds, and Magnus would lie in his bed and listen for them until he dropped off to sleep.

"I don't *want* to go away from here," he said emphatically.

5

His mother made no reply, she was too busy wrapping up glass and china and packing it in a tea chest which stood in the middle of the room. Magnus heaved a sigh and walked slowly down the stairs. His feet were bare because it was nearly midsummer now and very hot indeed. Matthew had said it was a heat wave, and Father had told him that it hadn't been as hot as this in fifty years. Mother exclaimed that if they didn't get some rain soon she'd give up the ghost. Magnus had asked her what she meant by "give up the ghost."

6

"Well, I suppose it means to fade away," she had said — hesitantly.

Magnus fervently hoped that Mother wouldn't fade away. He wouldn't mind if the move faded away though.

Although it was terribly hot outside, it was cold on the stairs. The steps were made of stone and the street noises echoed faintly on the staircase. In the old days Magnus used to shout, "Oo! Oo!" on the stairs, because it made such a beautiful echo. But he didn't do it any more; he was eight now — not a small child any longer, and he had grown out of that sort of thing. He wasn't the smallest in the class any more and all spring he had been a member of the Cathedral Gang.

It was quite a good gang to belong to, even though he had sometimes got rather fed up with the other boys and girls. The never stopped arguing, and each one wanted to take the lead. It made Magnus feel out of sorts, he hated to hear them quarreling. He much preferred to wander around and explore. It was fun to prowl around on stairs, and among wooden boxes and tea chests in attics, especially when it was getting dark; it was all the more creepy and exciting then. You could flit across a courtyard, up into an attic, out on a roof, and come down onto a different street. There were cellars that had long passages, and when you explored them you didn't know where you were going to end up. Sometimes big boys chased you along the street, and if they caught up with you, they might lock you up in one of these dark cellars.

Although Magnus was really fed up with the fights and squabbles, he didn't want to go away from here. In the block where he lived there were no other children; there were only offices and stores, and Mr. Bergstrom's paper-and-cardboard storeroom. That was where Matthew worked as a delivery boy. But there were no children at all for Magnus to play with. That was why he had become one of the Cathedral Gang, otherwise he woud have been all on his own.

But in the spring some of them had moved, and the others must have joined other gangs. Again, Magnus was standing alone in the archway, looking out onto the street — with no one to play with. Matthew was still there, of course, but he had his job. He raced about on his motorcycle with paper and envelopes, and he had to collect money from the bank and from the customers.

Magnus quickly continued down the cold stairs and ran into the sun-drenched courtyard. It was so hot and stuffy out there that you could hardly breathe for gasoline fumes and dust. Mr. Andersson, whose job it was to keep the courtyard clean, had swept up every single matchstick, so Magnus couldn't find even one for tracing the outlines of the cobblestones.

He squatted in the courtyard. The hot stones burned the

bare soles of his feet. "There's nothing to do," he muttered. "I want a dog!"

He got up and shouted at the top of his voice, "I want a dog!"

A car passed in the street, an airplane zoomed in the sky, a butterfly fluttered past. Nothing else happened.

Magnus filled his lungs with air.

"I want a dog," he yelled till he was blue in the face. "I want it at once!" he added more quickly, because he was getting hoarse with shouting.

Mr. Andersson opened his window and looked out.

"What's all this racket going on down there?" he demanded.

Magnus didn't answer. Instead, he got up and went under the archway. There he lay down right across the entrance from the street and watched the passers-by from below. He saw sandals and shoes, he saw billowing, brightly-colored skirts, and trousers with patches in them. Then he saw a pair of chubby little legs — the owner couldn't be more than three years old, he thought. In the street there was a constant stream of cars and motorcycles, all going in the same direction, because this was a one-way street.

With a mournful voice Magnus began to chant:

> *I want a dog to be my friend,*
> *a dog who would my walks attend;*

9

a faithful dog is always true,
and would my every wish pursue.

Magnus thought that the melancholy song was just right, everything was perfectly horrid: having to leave the kitchen he liked, not having a dog, and not having anybody to play with.

At that moment Matthew came zooming along on his motorcycle. He swerved into the gateway and stopped within and inch of Magnus's head.

"What sort of a place is this for lying down?" he asked severely.

"I want a dog," said Magnus, pouting.

"Is that a way to get a dog?" asked Matthew.

"I don't know. I'm trying it out," answered Magnus.

"Well! I'll try my luck too, then," said Matthew.

He propped his motorcycle against the wall and before Magnus had time to think, Matthew had taken off his leather jacket and lay stretched out across the gateway. Matthew was so tall that he could lean his head against one wall and his feet against the other. People were beginning to stop in front of the gateway to watch the two boys lying there.

Matthew was seventeen this summer and had grown a little mustache. Magnus thought it looked silly, but in every other way Matthew was still like a big brother to him: just the same as ever. He wasn't his real brother, though. He had his

own father and mother living in the country up towards
Kings River, but he looked upon himself as Magnus's big
brother, because he had his lunch at Magnus's home every
day, and the two boys spent a lot of their time together.

By now there was quite a crowd outside, watching Magnus and Matthew.

"Are they dead?" asked a small child.

"Someone must phone for the ambulance," said an elderly lady.

"What's going on here?" spoke a voice of authority — no doubt a policeman.

In an instant Magnus and Matthew were on their feet. Matthew seized the motorcycle, Magnus grabbed the leather jacket, and the next moment they were safely inside Mr. Bergstrom's storeroom. From the window they watched to see if the policeman would come into the courtyard, but he didn't.

"So we didn't get a dog, after all," said Matthew. "Bad luck!"

"Ah well, never mind," replied Magnus. "They won't let you keep a dog in this courtyard, anyway, there's something in the lease about it."

"I don't think they'll let you keep a dog where you're moving to either," remarked Matthew.

"I don't want to move," stated Magnus defiantly. "I'm not going to, I'm staying here."

"Okay," said Matthew. "You stay, but I'm going home for my vacation, and afterwards I'm starting a job at a stationer's in Kings River. I'm going to go to evening classes there, so I can learn to be a manager, and later I shall have my own store."

Magnus looked up in astonishment.

"Aren't you going to be a delivery boy any longer?" he

asked, with alarm in his voice. "You're not going to leave Mr. Bergstrom's, are you?"

"Oh yes, surely you didn't think I was going to be a delivery boy all my life till I'm an old man with a long beard? I don't think I'd like that very much!"

Magnus couldn't help laughing at the thought, but he felt, in fact, more like crying. If only he hadn't been eight years old he probably would have cried, first of all because he, himself, was going to move away, and secondly because Matthew was.

Slowly he walked out into the courtyard.

There he sat down on the cobblestones to think. "If only I had a dog," he thought, "then the dog would be with me all the time, and now that I have to move, the dog would have to come, too. I shouldn't mind so much about moving if I went there with a dog of my own."

"What're you mumbling about?" asked Matthew's voice beside him.

"I'm completely fed up!" said Magnus frankly.

"Rubbish," said Matthew, "it won't be as bad as you think."

Magnus was silent.

"No," he thought rebelliously, "it won't be as bad as I think to move to a place where I don't know anybody, and where they don't know me — Why, anything might happen there, you can't tell! Oh no! It won't be as bad as I think, losing Matthew and not having a big brother any more. Great fun, that's what it'll be! And not having a dog to go with — that's not so bad either, I suppose!"

He opened his mouth and shut his eyes tight.

"*I want a dog!*" he screamed so loudly it was surprising that the traffic on East Hamn Street didn't come to a standstill. Two small children, who were standing by the gateway, looking into the courtyard, burst into tears.

Mr. Andersson threw his window open.

"This racket is driving me crazy!" he roared.

Mother, too, opened her window.

"What on earth's happening to you?" she called.

Matthew came rushing out of Mr. Bergstrom's storeroom.

"Not much wrong with your lungs!" he remarked. "You'd be a useful person to have around the harbor when there's a fog!"

It wasn't a very nice thing for a big brother to say, but Matthew was smiling, and Magnus didn't mind.

"Where are you going?" asked Magnus with a sigh when he saw Matthew putting his helmet on.

"To Hising Island with an envelope," replied Matthew, "and after I've delivered it, I think I shall go home for my lunch. Would you like to come?" Magnus nodded.

"Quickly then, get your leather jacket and put your shoes on. I'll wait for you."

Mr. Andersson shut his window with a bang as Magnus

14

ran upstairs, two at a time.

"That's a good idea," said his mother when he told her that he was going on the motorcycle with Matthew. "But don't be back late, we're having dinner at half-past six because Father is going with the first truck load tonight."

Magnus nodded. He certainly didn't feel very happy, but there was nothing he could do, either about Matthew going away or about himself going away.

A little later, when he was sitting behind Matthew on the back of the motorcycle, zooming out through the arched gateway, his spirits rose.

15

2

A Ride
with Mr. Lindberg

THERE is nothing quite like riding on a motorcycle. When
you travel in a car you're sitting inside a little compartment,
and you simply glide along — it's quite pleasant, but it's not
like riding on a motorcycle! You're right out in the open
then, and it's so easy to get along! You just shoot past the
cars and trams with only an inch to spare on each side of you.
There's always a cool breeze in your hair and around your
legs, even in the worst heat wave.

Matthew had been a delivery boy for such a long time that
there was nothing he didn't know about motorcycles. He
never made a dreadful noise like some riders who seem to

enjoy not using the muffler. Quietly, Matthew would weave his way between the trucks and buses. Sometimes the gap was so narrow that Magnus felt he must pull himself tightly together so that he wouldn't get squashed, but they always arrived safely, and in record time. Going around the bends, Magnus sometimes thought he could easily have touched the road if he had stretched out his hand.

Magnus kept a firm grip on Matthew's waist, and he wasn't a bit frightened. He was used to going on the motorcycle with Matthew, and not only in the city. They had traveled in the country, too — along narrow lanes where you jogged up and down so much that it seemed you spent more time up in the air than down on the seat of the motorcycle. The whole of your inside felt as if it was being whisked, like scrambling eggs. Matthew had a safety belt strapped around him when he went for long distances into the country. But Magnus didn't have one — not yet, anyway. Once they had gone across a field covered with snow. Again and again they had skidded, and each time the snow had blown up like a cloud around them. In the end, Matthew had lost control over the steering, the motorcycle fell over, and when the two boys got up out of the snow they looked for all the world like snowmen — it was good fun! Afterwards they went straight home, and Magnus's mother gave them hot chocolate to drink, which made them feel warm and cozy inside. Come to think of it, Magnus always felt like that going on the motorcycle with Matthew.

Now, as they traveled down East Hamn Street on their way to Hising Bridge, Magnus was grinning with pleasure. Soon they came upon a traffic jam. It was the line of vehicles waiting to cross the bridge. All the shipping up and down the Gotha River and Canal has to pass, either under the bridge, or, in the case of big ships, between the raised spans. So, at intervals, the bridge is closed to traffic while the spans are raised. Very rapidly, a line forms, and before long it stretches right down into the city. With little splutterings from the motorcycle, Matthew edged forward. The spans were closing, but it would be a minute or two before the barriers were raised. Above, the sky was a deep blue, and the seagulls were wheeling around, squawking. Below, the water in the harbor glittered, and on all sides rose the green hills of Gothenburg.

Now the barriers went up.

"Hold tight!" shouted Matthew.

Magnus took a firmer grip as they slipped under the barriers and raced out on to the long bridge which leads to Hising Island. Soon most of the other vehicles were far behind them, and Matthew had his side of the bridge almost to himself.

Matthew was making for Ring Island. They had to wait a moment for the lights to change, then they were on their way again to that part of Hising Island which is called Ring

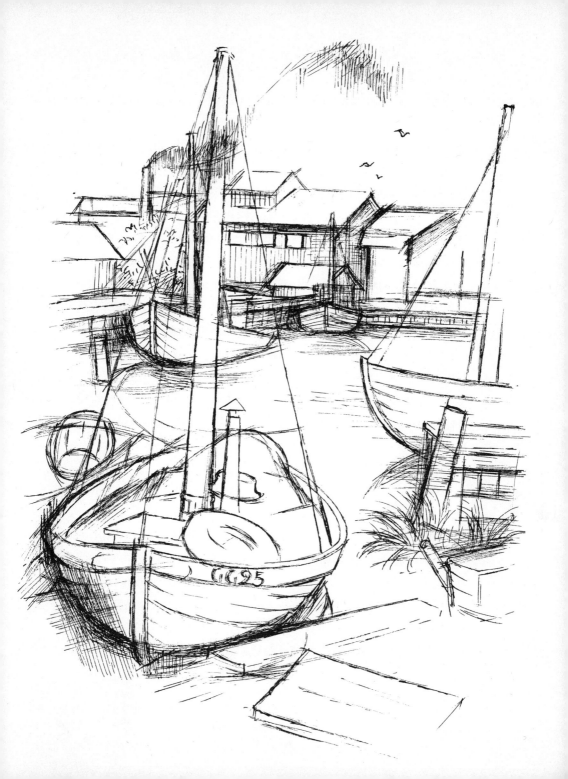

Island, though it isn't a real island. It faces the river and is full of factories, large and small ones. The railway line to Free harbor runs across it, and there are lots of little bushes and dried-up trees and a wharf for small boats. There are many derelict skiffs lying about and some pretty queer characters live here — people who don't want to live in a real house, people who want to keep themselves to themselves, also some who don't want the police to know their whereabouts. It's simply asking for trouble to walk around on Ring Island after dark. Anything can happen then.

But in the daytime it's good fun down there. Ring Island looks quite pleasant then, and it's interesting to wander round, looking at the wrecks of old boats full of rubbish, rats, and other weird things.

Just as Matthew and Magnus were shooting down the wide street, lined with factories, they spotted a horse-drawn wagon. At once Matthew stopped the motorcycle.

"Hi, Mr. Lindberg!" called Magnus.

"Why! If it isn't Magnus and his big brother coming along as if ten devils were at their heels!" exclaimed Mr. Lindberg, twiddling his drooping mustache. "It's enough to frighten honest folk out of their wits!"

"Why is it only honest folk that are frightened out of their wits?" asked Matthew with a smile and with a twinkle in his eye.

"Ah, you've got me there," replied Mr. Lindberg. "I sup-

pose the others are just used to being frightened, that's the long and short of it."

Magnus had by now jumped down from the motorcycle and gone over to the old brown horse whose name was Mary. It was some months now since Mr. Lindberg had been taken suddenly ill. Matthew and Magnus had rescued Mary from Northtown where she had been standing in a stable which was about to be pulled down. During a bitter winter's night, and with grim adventures on the way, they had taken her to safety in a stable beyond the opposite end of the city, way out in the country. So Magnus and Mary were old friends, and while Matthew and Mr. Lindberg were discussing "honest folk," Magnus and Mary had their own discussion. Now he found it hard to believe that, once, he had not dared go near enough to her to give her a lump of sugar.

"Mr. Lindberg!" he called. "Have you some sugar I could give her?"

"Take a look in this box," answered Mr. Lindberg.

Magnus looked and found a small bag of sugar. He took out two lumps which he gave to Mary. She nodded her old head and gently ate them from Magnus's hand.

"And what's your errand this time?" Mr. Lindberg asked Matthew.

"I've got to deliver a hundred and fifty dollars," replied Matthew.

At this he pulled the motorcycle towards him, because two fellows, who had been coming along the road, seemed about to walk into it. They walked on, but not until they'd taken a good look at Matthew.

"So Magnus has come to keep me company," continued Matthew.

"Yes, it's nice to have someone to talk to. I always have Mary, and I'd say she's better company than a rattly old tin can," said Mr. Lindberg with an expressive look towards the motorcycle.

Matthew laughed heartily.

"I don't know about that," said Matthew. "There are times when I talk to my motorcycle. 'Speed up, now!' I tell her, and perhaps you won't believe me when I say it, but I'll be darned if it doesn't work: she goes like the wind."

"That may be so," said Mr. Lindberg, nodding his head, "but I just don't see any sense in having them new-fangled mechanical things. I'm too old, I daresay, but I'd sooner have Mary to talk to any day than a rattlesnaky contraption like that. We've all got a right to our own ideas, though."

Matthew just smiled and made no comment. There *was* something in what Mr. Lindberg said. Matthew pulled a handkerchief out of his pocket and stuffed it into the space between the number plate and the mudguard. It did rattle a bit now that he thought about it.

"I think we'd better be on our way," he called to Magnus.

"Mr. Lindberg!" asked Magnus. "Why don't you come to Mr. Bergstrom's storeroom any more? It was great fun going on the wagon with you."

"I enjoyed it myself, having you to talk to," answered Mr. Lindberg smiling. "But it looks as if it will be a long time before I can come that way again. I have plenty of work around here. Right now I've got to collect twenty-three crates of bananas from a place over there. Pity I hadn't already done it when you came along, then I could have given you a banana each."

"Couldn't I stay and help you till Matthew comes back?" asked Magnus.

"That's okay with me," said Matthew and started his

23

motorcycle. "It may take longer than I think, but I shouldn't be more than ten minutes at the most," and he was gone.

Magnus climbed up on the wagon beside Mr. Lindberg. Mary raised her tired old head and trotted off. They went in the opposite direction from Matthew. Magnus heaved a sigh of contentment. There is nothing that compares with riding on a motorcycle. But there isn't anything quite like sitting beside Mr. Lindberg on top of a wagon, either — especially if the wagon is pulled along by old Mary, and you can see her heaving, dark brown back just in front of you. All too soon they reached the place where Mr. Lindberg had to pick up the crates of bananas. Magnus asked Mr. Lindberg if he could spend the rest of the day with him on the wagon — if Matthew didn't mind, of course.

"I don't see why not," answered Mr. Lindberg, as he went into a gateway to fetch the first crate.

Mary pulled at the reins as she lowered her head. She looked as if she wanted to take a nap. The sun was beating down — it was as hot as in a steam bath. Magnus could hear the honking of cars from the bridge and the squawks of seagulls. Mr. Lindberg heaved one crate after another onto the wagon with the help of Magnus who called out to Mary each time he returned to the wagon.

"Can't think what's happened to that boy," exclaimed Mr. Lindberg suddenly, and Magnus realized that Matthew must have been gone for much longer than ten minutes.

Magnus went to the corner of the block and had a look, but there was no sign of Matthew and no sound of his motorcycle, either.

Mr. Lindberg had finished loading the crates and had climbed up on the wagon. He had given Magnus four bananas, two for himself and two for Matthew.

"I'm afraid I must go, I'll have to leave you here. If I were to take you with me, and Matthew came back and couldn't find you, he would be worried."

Magnus nodded. He felt rather annoyed with Matthew — he'd promised to be back in ten minutes, and now Magnus couldn't go with Mr. Lindberg on the wagon for the rest of the day. Mary raised her head, and her big brown eyes looked benevolently down on Magnus. Then, slowly, she began to clop away towards the bridge.

Magnus stood and watched until the wagon disappeared in the distance, then he started to eat a banana. It tasted so good after the ride through the city on the motorcycle and then on the wagon with Mr. Lindberg, that Magnus decided to eat his second banana as well. Suddenly he caught sight of a dog — a very big dog — well, to begin with Magnus thought it must be a pony, but when he looked more closely he could see from the tail and paws that it was a dog all right. Magnus crossed his fingers, hoping that Matthew would turn up before the dog came much closer to him. It wasn't that he was afraid of dogs, not really. Matthew had told him sev-

25

eral times that they never bite if you stay put. But with a dog as big as this, well . . . how could you be sure? Besides, how were you to know that the dog would notice whether you were staying put or going to run away from it? He fervently hoped *it* would run away from *him*, or else that Matthew would arrive at once. He usually did turn up at the right moment.

The dog was now coming closer and closer. Magnus could see it had a thick brown coat with white spots. It also had a broad head, and a long red tongue was hanging out of its mouth. "It must be terrible to have such a thick coat on such a hot day," thought Magnus.

26

In that instant he heard the most welcome sound in the world: there was no mistaking the chugging noise of Matthew's motorcycle. Magnus moved over to the street corner. Now he could see the motorcycle all right, coming along the street — Matthew must have taken his helmet off because of the heat. He was going along at a very high speed, faster than usual. Magnus remained where he was, at first a little surprised, then more and more surprised, in the end he was so astounded that he could do nothing but stare.

It was Matthew's motorcycle all right; he had just time to catch sight of the number plate as it roared past him, but it wasn't Matthew who was sitting on it! Matthew had red hair, and, in the summer, he had freckles. He had his hair cut short, too, far under his helmet. This fellow on the motorcycle was much older, he had hair hanging down the back of his neck and was wearing an ordinary suit.

Magnus stood rooted to the ground and stared after him. For a moment he thought he must be dreaming, he had to pinch himself to find out. Oh no, he was awake all right, he was standing beside a brick wall on Ring Island, and Matthew had disappeared. Someone had stolen Matthew's motorcycle. And, what was more, the dog, big as a pony, was slowly but surely moving towards him.

3

Max

MAGNUS stood still for a long time, his head felt quite empty.

"I want to go home," he said softly.

He remembered hearing someone say this once, he'd forgotten who it was, but perhaps it was somebody who felt small and lonely. Of course, Magnus didn't feel small and lonely, but he felt very much like going home. It was a long way home, and he couldn't very well go without letting Matthew know. For a moment it occurred to him to rush off to try and catch up with Mr. Lindberg, but it was too late for that. Mr. Lindberg had been gone too long, and would have got too far.

28

Suddenly Magnus realized that he was staring into a pair of yellow eyes above a huge mouth that was so big you could have stuck your head into it. From out of this gaping mouth hung a long, red, trembling tongue.

Magnus edged back towards the brick wall; the big dog moved, too.

"This is just fine," thought Magnus, "he's going to eat me up. Then there won't be either a Matthew or a Magnus left, and Father and Mother will have to move by themselves . . ." Magnus felt quite sad at the thought.

The dog sat down with his nose very close to Magnus. He seemed to want to take a good look at his dinner before he swallowed it. Magnus pressed himself flat against the wall and looked right and left for someone to come to his rescue. But his frightened eyes scanned the empty street in vain.

"Well!" thought Magnus. "You'd expect there would be at least a policeman around, if no one else, to make sure people don't get eaten up by big dogs."

He stepped to one side. Immediately the big dog got up, and Magnus's heart leaped to his throat. "Something must be done about this," Matthew would say.

"Something must be done about this," thought Magnus.

"But what? I could easily drop down dead, but as I don't seem to I can't be all that frightened." Then he turned to the dog and said quietly, "Hello, fellow!"

The dog closed his great jaws and put his head to one side,

watching Magnus with melancholy eyes.

"Say! Supposing you go *that* way and I go *this* way?" suggested Magnus, pointing simultaneously in opposite directions.

The dog gave a bark. It sounded to Magnus as though the house behind him had crumbled. He shut his eyes, quite expecting to drop down dead. When he opened them again he found the dog sitting down, sniffing at the bananas which Magnus was holding in his hand. Magnus tentatively held one out to him. Cautiously, as though it were made of china, the dog took it, placed it on the sidewalk, and sniffed at it. Then he wagged his tail and looked at Magnus with imploring eyes.

"Oh yes!" nodded Magnus, "I'll peel it for you, I'm sure glad I've eaten mine, though. If you're going to eat Matthew's bananas, he won't like that very much, but I suppose you'll have to now."

He peeled the bananas, one after the other, and all the time the dog's tail wagged to and fro. The dog swallowed the bananas whole, leaving not a trace. After that it licked its chops with its enormous red tongue. Magnus patted the dog on the head, rather gingerly at first, then he started to stroke him, and finally he put his arm around the dog.

"You should wear a label on you to say that you're a tame dog," continued Magnus. "It's a waste for people to die of fright just from looking at you."

As he spoke, the dog's tail kept wagging, and then the dog began to lick Magnus all over his face.

"I'd rather wash my own face, thank you all the same," said Magnus.

"How could I have been afraid of this dog?" he thought. Now he remembered Matthew saying that small dogs are sometimes fierce, but big dogs hardly ever are.

"I know what!" Magnus burst out. "We'll go looking for Matthew together! You never know what we might run into, and it's much better to be two than one when there is trouble brewing."

The dog nodded his head as though in full agreement.

"But what shall I call you? Let me think . . . If I had a dog as big as you I'd call him Max — you look like a Max, big and trustworthy — but I haven't, worse luck! It's in the lease about not being allowed to keep a dog on the block where I live."

Max got up and started walking down the street just as though he thought that this wasn't the proper time to talk about the lease. Magnus followed.

Now that he was no longer afraid of Max, he began to worry about Matthew again. He looked up and down the street, but still there was no sign of a policeman — or of anyone, for that matter. Magnus took a firm grip on the dog's coat and, staying as much as possible in the shadow of the houses, the two of them cautiously made their way in the direction from which Matthew's motorcycle had come — with the unknown rider.

In this part of Hising Island there are not only buildings along the streets, but also yards fenced in with wooden boardings. There are hardly any trees, only low bushes, and further along, some big garbage dumps. Magnus and Max continued walking along the wide street. Once a truck passed them, then a small red car. Max stayed close to Magnus.

Magnus felt much safer now that he had a dog at his side. It was sort of like having a big brother beside you. At times Max stopped in his tracks as though he were afraid to go on, but Magnus patted him reassuringly on the head.

"Don't worry!" said Magnus. "I'm here, and when there are two of you, there's nothing to be afraid of. You see, we can help each other! That's what Matthew and I do. Well . . . really it's mostly Matthew who helps me."

Yes, Matthew! What could have happened to him? Had he stopped somewhere on the way, left his motorcycle for a moment and come back to find it gone? But then he would have come to fetch Magnus who was waiting for him . . .

As they turned the corner into a narrow road which led towards a railroad track, Magnus spotted something white lying on the ground. When they came closer to it, Magnus saw that it was a handkerchief. Max went up to it, took one sniff at it and continued on his way. But Magnus stopped and picked it up. Why it looked like Matthew's! Magnus remembered quite clearly seeing Matthew stuff his handkerchief in between the number plate and the mudguard to stop the rattling. Magnus sat down on the edge of the sidewalk and Max came back and sat down beside him.

There was nothing that Magnus wanted to do more than to turn around and make straight for home. It was nice to have Max there beside him — though it would have been better still if Max had been his own dog — and it was quite pleasant sitting here. At least it wasn't cold, and he'd had two big bananas to eat, he wasn't going to die of starvation. Everything was pretty well all right, everything except that

Matthew had vanished without a trace.

If only he were at home, he thought, sitting on the cobbles in the courtyard and Matthew coming zooming in through the gateway, shouting: "Hi, Magnus! How's everything?" Magnus liked it when Matthew showed up suddenly like that when he least expected it. And if Matthew didn't come driving in when Magnus was sitting in the courtyard, Magnus could always go up to Mother and call out: "Hi! How about a nice cold drink of orange juice and one of your delicious doughnuts?"

That's what Father always said, and Magnus liked the sound of it. It made Mother laugh, and sometimes she would fetch the orange juice and the doughnuts. At other times she would say that it was nearly dinnertime and it would spoil his appetite — and would he mind going down to the dairy for a quart of milk — then dinner would be on the table when he got back. Father would run down the cold stairs and out into the hot courtyard. Magnus liked everything at home; you always *knew* what was going to happen.

Here he was far from home, together with a dog he called Max (but he had no idea of his real name), and who could tell? Maybe any moment now the dog would take it into his head to run away and leave Magnus all alone.

"You wouldn't leave me, would you?" pleaded Magnus.

Max stretched out his right paw as if to say, "How-do-you-do?" You could tell he had been very well brought up.

Magnus took his paw and kissed his cold, wet, black nose. Then he looked up and down the street. There was no one about. Only on the main street he could see a truck passing now and then, but they all seemed to be in a great hurry. It wasn't any use trying to stop one of them . . . well, if he went and stood out in the middle of the road perhaps he could. . . . But what would he say if it stopped? "Hi! I'm Magnus, and Matthew — who's like a big brother to me — has disappeared."

The driver would only say: "I expect he's playing hide-and-seek with you, young fellow!" slam in his gears, put his foot down on the accelerator, and be gone.

"Hide-and-seek! Indeed!" thought Magnus. If only it wasn't vacation time he could ask his schoolteacher what to do. It was true she had a big class, but Magnus knew that she would let him talk to her in the corridor if he asked her, and she would listen carefully to what he had to say. She would put a finger to her cheek, frown thoughtfully and say: "Let's see what we can do about it!"

Then she would be silent for a little time, and while she was thinking, you could hear the children in the other classrooms answering questions, and the water gurgling in the pipes along the corridor. Then she would say just the right thing to help you and take you back to the classroom, and you wouldn't be worried any more.

But the summer vacations were here, and nobody knew

where the teacher had gone to. When you stopped to think of it, everybody disappeared just when you wanted them. Father would have scratched his head, then he would have called Mother, and the three of them would have tackled the problem together. But Father was at work, and Mother was packing, so in a way she, too, had disappeared.

Suddenly Magnus got up — he had an idea.

"Matthew's handkerchief!" he said to Max and held it to the dog's nose. "Track him down! Track him down!"

Max wagged his tail, and immediately he set off with quick loping strides. Magnus looked after him in astonishment. Max seemed to understand.

4

Meeting Veronica

AFTER taking a few strides, Max stopped, waiting for Magnus to catch him up. When they came to a bend in the road, Magnus saw some men in blue overalls, working in a railway yard. But there was no sign of Matthew. Then Magnus followed a red-painted fence, and suddenly Max disappeared through a hole in the fence. After taking one more look for Matthew, Magnus, too, crept through the hole.

On the other side of the fence there was an odd assortment of old cars of every type; most of them were so ancient that they barely held together. Quite a few of them had no tires; others had no windows. The doors were crooked, and the

upholstery inside the cars was in shreds.

Max looked around, then he sat down. Magnus immediately started to look inside the broken-down cars. Perhaps Matthew had lost his way in this jumble, or perhaps he was looking for a car to buy and had become so interested that he had forgotten that Magnus was waiting for him. But that wasn't the kind of thing Matthew would do.

Magnus went from one car to the next, with Max following close on his heels. They went into a bus, but quickly retreated; two cats which had been asleep in a corner did not exactly welcome the presence of a dog on their premises, and Max was the first to get out and away from the hissing of those creatures with arched backs. Suddenly Magnus heard the sound of voices. With a firm grip on Max's coat he moved cautiously in their direction, but Max freed himself and, before Magnus could stop him, rushed ahead with his tail wagging furiously.

In the corner of the big enclosure stood a trailer which looked like an old railroad car. Below it was a sandpit; in it sat a little girl who kept filling her pail with the fine sand and emptying it over her head. Each time she shook her head vigorously, and the sand flew in all directions. On the steps of the trailer sat a man reading a newspaper, and beside him stood a girl with gold hair. Max was wagging his tail furiously; in fact, his entire body seemed to be wagging with pleasure.

Magnus looked on for a while, then he turned to go. So Max was not a retriever after all, as he had thought. Max had taken one sniff at Matthew's handkerchief and run straight home! Magnus cast one more glance at the caravan. "Lucky people," he thought, "living in a trailer. You needn't stay in one place all the time, and yet you keep your own house — best of all, you can have a dog anytime you want one, no

matter how big!"

"Hello!" called the girl. "Thank you for bringing Max home."

Magnus was so intrigued by the way in which the girl spoke, pronouncing each syllable very distinctly, and pausing between every word, he did not realize that she was calling the dog "Max." She had dimples in her cheeks, and she smiled all the time. She looked so very nice and friendly that Magnus didn't feel shy at all. She would be about his own age, he thought, but the little girl in the sandpit couldn't be more than three. She was now picking grains of sand out of her hair.

"I think it was *Max* who brought me here, not *me* that brought him home," said Magnus, when they all looked at him as though they expected him to say something.

"Stay and play with me for a while, won't you?" said the girl pleadingly in her strange monotonous voice. Magnus didn't know what to say; he would have liked to stay and play with her if it hadn't been for Matthew. The man put his paper aside and stood up.

"I'm always very glad when Veronica has someone to play with," he said. "You see, she can't hear, but she can see from the way you move your lips what you're saying."

He went over to a heap of car lights, broken glass, tires, and mirrors.

"I get a number of old cars coming in every day," he continued. "It's my job to break them up and sort out the good parts. You'd be surprised what a lot there is that can be salvaged."

"Boy!" called Veronica. "You're not to old to play in the sandpit, are you?"

Magnus looked down, thinking. Of course he was really much too old. He was used to going on a motorcycle, he was old enough to build a hut in the forest (if there had been a forest to build a hut in) but she looked as though she would be awfully happy if he would play and she looked so nice,

41

with her golden hair.

"No-o, I don't think I'm too old. I'd like to play with you, but I mustn't stay long," answered Magnus.

The girl took his chin and raised his head.

"What did you say?" she asked.

Slowly and carefully Magnus repeated what he had said, and all the time the girl watched his lips. Then she smiled happily and danced off towards the sandpit. The little girl looked up and smiled shyly at Magnus.

"Hi," Magnus said to her.

She was so overcome by shyness that she pressed the pail down hard over her head. A second later she began to scream; the pail had got stuck. Her father came running, and all three of them helped to remove the pail from the little girl's head. She laughed and went on picking grains of sand out of her hair.

It was quite a big sandpit, and before long Magnus and Veronica had built a tower and a fortress with high walls around it. Now and then, Magnus looked around to see if anyone was watching him. Supposing one of the Cathedral Gang caught sight of him — they would think it babyish — he would never live it down. But Matthew would have been down on his hands and knees, helping — that was the best thing about Matthew, he never thought you childish, you could be yourself with him. Playing in a sandpit was very agreeable, really, with none of all that squabbling that went

on in the gang. And Matthew . . .

In an instant Magnus was on his feet. He had heard the sound of a motorcycle; perhaps it was Matthew's? How could he settle down to play in a sandpit, while all the time Matthew must be going around, searching for him? Veronica, too, got up, and now she was looking at Magnus with questioning eyes.

"My big brother," explained Magnus. "He is looking for me."

Without another word, he turned and ran through the maze of cars towards the fence. He took a dive through the hole, then stopped dead in his tracks. The motorcycle! Matthew's! Magnus could see the number plate. It was leaning up against a lamppost. But the boy beside it was the dark haired fellow!

He caught sight of Magnus as he quietly made his retreat through the hole. Max had followed Magnus, and together they watched while the boy lit a cigarette and slowly walked away, looking back over his shoulder from time to time until he disappeared among some shacks next to the railroad line.

At once Magnus slipped back through the hole. Yes! It was Matthew's motorcycle, all right. He looked hopefully for a policeman or some other grown-up to whom he could tell what had happened, and who could put everything right. But, of course, nobody came, not so much as a cat. Not that a cat would have been much use, anyway, when not even Max, who was sitting beside him panting in the heat, could do anything about it. It surprised Magnus that Max had not stayed behind with Veronica and her father and sister by the caravan.

As Magnus stood looking at the motorcycle, he had an idea. Good! It wasn't locked; he pushed it off the supports and wheeled it along the street. It was very heavy; before Magnus had reached the corner of the road, he was dripping with perspiration. He had to keep an eye open, too, in case the dark haired fellow came running back. But he seemed to be gone for the time being, and Magnus managed to push the heavy motorcycle around the corner toward the entrance to the junk yard.

44

"Goodness!" he thought anxiously. "I hope I shall manage it in time. I promise to be as good as gold for years and years if only I can manage to get the motorcycle to Veronica's in time."

He was getting closer; soon he stood, once more, by the sandpit.

"What on earth have you got there?" exclaimed Veronica's father, getting up.

"Is it yours?" asked Veronica shyly, watching with her large eyes.

45

The little girl with the sand in her hair came up and gave Magnus a big smile.

"You're nice," she said. "I like you!"

Quickly Magnus explained to the man that Matthew had disappeared, and that his motorcycle had been stolen, and that this was it.

"What are we going to do with it?" asked Veronica.

"We've got to hide it, so that the thief can't find it," said Magnus breathlessly. "He might be back any minute!"

"We ought to call the police," said her father, "but we haven't got a phone, worse luck."

"We've got to be quick!" said Magnus, still out of breath. "He may be along at any moment — the boy who stole it."

The man nodded, and the three of them — he, Veronica, and Magnus — pushed the motorcycle over to a bus, lifted it in, and shut the door firmly.

When they returned to the sandpit they found the dark haired fellow standing there. He looked furious and cast angry glances at Magnus.

"My motorcycle's gone!" he blurted out.

"Well . . . there's plenty of dishonest folk about, worse luck!" remarked Veronica's father.

Veronica had been tugging at Magnus, and they had both gone into the trailer. Now they were standing by the window, watching.

"It wouldn't be anywhere around these parts, would it by

46

any chance?" asked the boy.

"Not to my knowledge, it wouldn't," they heard Veronica's father say. "We've got an old bike or two, I daresay, but I wouldn't know if yours is there amongst them. What's it like? What's the number, anyway?"

"Well...it's...it's new, actually," answered the boy, waveringly. "I can't remember it quite, haven't had time yet to learn the number...hmm...I think it was..."

"Oh!" exclaimed Veronica's father as if it had just dawned on him, "then it's got the number in red!"

"No, it was white," answered the fellow.

"But as far as I can remember they always have the new numbers in red. By the time people have a white number plate, they've had plenty of time to learn the number, I should think."

"It's been gone less than five minutes," shouted the dark haired fellow, and now he sounded awfully angry. "It can't have got far yet."

"Oh, I see," said Veronica's father. "Then it shouldn't be at all difficult to track the thief down. Why didn't you say that right away? I'll call the police so that they can get on to him at once. One can't let people get away with that sort of thing while honest folk have to scrape and save from their earnings to buy a bike. Yes! I'll see about phoning the police."

"We haven't got a telephone," whispered Veronica to Magnus, but her father was marching briskly toward the

47

door of the trailer. The boy caught up with him and blocked the way.

"I think I'd better have a good look around myself first," he stammered. "It mightn't be far off," and with this he dashed off into the street. Veronica's father closed the big gates behind him.

"Just a moment! He ain't goin' to shut them gates right in the face of an ole man, is he?"

Magnus looked up in astonishment towards the gate, and Veronica, seeing the expression on his face, asked, "Is somebody coming?"

"Yes," said Magnus, "somebody with a voice like a fog horn."

"Oh!" exclaimed Veronica, "I know who it is! It's Captain Lillem!"

She ran down the path and nearly collided with an old man who was wearing a peaked cap on top of his gray head and carrying a stick in his hand.

Veronica's father was laughing as he said to Magnus, "You have the motorcycle safely tucked away. Now what about finding Matthew?"

"Were you really going to call the police?" asked Magnus.

"Oh no! I was just putting him to a test — if he had thought it a good idea, he might have been an honest fellow. He could have bought the motorcycle from someone who had stolen it from Matthew. You see, we should never jump to conclusions."

"You're wrong there," interrupted Skipper Lillem. "You should always expect the worst — thieves and robbers, the whole lot of 'em — they ain't landlubbers for nothin'. Bloomin' pack of rascals!"

"I'd better be off right away," said Magnus, "I've got to find my big brother — he's disappeared."

"Disappeared, has he?" exclaimed Captain Lillem. "What did I tell you? Just what you might expect from them land-lubbers! Do nothin' but disappear, leave no trace, know nothin' of law and order, the whole lot of 'em."

"Matthew isn't a bit like that," said Magnus staunchly. "He went off on his motorcycle, carrying a hundred and fifty dollars with him to pay a bill, and he didn't come back."

"One hundred and fifty dollars!" repeated Skipper Lillem slowly, ". . . and he never came back?"

"No," answered Magnus, "and I must find him."

"So you've got to find 'im, eh?" said Skipper Lillem. "And where do you intend to start looking?"

"I don't know," answered Magnus.

He was cross with himself now for stopping to play in the sandpit. Why hadn't he gone to look for Matthew at once?

"You know these parts like the back of your hand," said Veronica's father to Captain Lillem. "After sixty years on and off there can't be many nooks and crannies you don't know, why don't you help him look?"

"Well . . ." came Captain Lillem's slow reply, "I'm not so sure . . . you've got to know where to start looking. There was that time when I had to find Africa — some cotton wool they wanted me to collect — and there wasn't a sign of Africa anywhere, complete disappeared, it had. It came to me in a flash that I'd just got to find it — but supposing the whole lot of it had been moved to some place else . . ."

Magnus edged himself towards the gates. He wasn't in the least bit interested in Africa.

"Hello there!" Captain Lillem's reminiscences had come to an end. "Where are you off to?"

"I just thought I'd better go and look for Matthew now," answered Magnus.

"What's the hurry?" asked Captain Lillem, scratching his beard.

Magnus thought there was plenty of hurry — goodness, the whole morning gone and not a trace of Matthew yet! He might have been taken prisoner and put in a cellar or in some shack. He was probably lying there now at this moment, tied up with rope, and waiting for someone to come to his rescue. And who was there to rescue him but Magnus? Magnus, who all the time had been playing in a sandpit and listening to an old skipper talking about Africa!

"I *am* in a hurry!" and Magnus sounded almost desperate.

"Well, well, nothing to worry about . . ." began the skipper.

"Nothing to worry about, indeed!" thought Magnus. "You've got to get down to things, that's what Father always says." So it was nothing to worry about that Matthew had vanished completely and been gone for ages, and that anything might have happened to him, and that Magnus had done nothing about it yet! Most likely there would be plenty to worry about if he didn't go off this very minute to search for him . . .

Without another word, Magnus turned and strode away.

5

Captain Lillem
on the Trail

"HEY there! Don't leave me behind!" shouted Captain Lillem. "I'll help you look. That fellow . . . what's his name — d'you like him?" he asked as he caught up with Magnus.

"He's called Matthew," answered Magnus. "Of course I like him, he's my big brother — well . . . nearly my big brother, anyway."

"He must be a good fellow then, nice change from them thieves and robbers — worth looking for, eh?"

As Magnus, with the talkative skipper behind him, reached the street, he turned around and saw Veronica and her little sister, waving to him.

"I'll come back one of these days," called Magnus. "If you want me to."

"*Oh yes!*" shouted Veronica. "Come back soon!"

Magnus nodded and went off with Captain Lillem.

Captain Lillem walked very fast, although he was old and used a stick. Magnus had to half-run to keep pace with him. Presently Max caught up with them, leaping and barking.

"Now let's think!" said Captain Lillem. "He got as far as this on his motorcycle with a hundred and fifty dollars. Then you saw this other fellow with the motorcycle, so something has happened to Matthew. He must've been taken prisoner. I can remember once in South America — you know where South America is, don't you?"

"Oh yes, I do," replied Magnus. He remembered South America very well from the map at school.

They hadn't started learning about America yet, but the teacher had pointed out the different continents, and South America, Magnus had noticed, was stuck onto North America by a thin string of land.

"And you went there?" said Magnus with a certain amount of awe in his voice.

"I did and all," replied the skipper. "Some country that! Far up the Amazon River I went — hot wasn't the word for it. If we'd had it as cool in our refrigerator as it's here today, there'd have been no cause for complaint. You'd only got to go out in the sun for a second, and right away you

53

sizzled like a rasher of bacon in a pan.

"We were in a fight with some Indians up there, they were armed with poisoned arrows. If you got one of them arrows in your flesh, you were dead as a doornail in three minutes, but we got used to that sort of thing — got the knack of dodging, see? If I'd been one of them big fellows, I wouldn't have been knocking around now, and you'd be here all on your own, looking for that fellow Matthew. You see, because

54

I wasn't all that big, I ran faster than the rest. I was sun-tanned, too, and that made the Indians think I was one of them.

"But once I got into a real scrape. The Indians were creeping up on us from all sides. We ran down to the river, but it was so full of snakes and crocodiles that there was hardly any water, let alone any room to swim. Luckily I'd brought the small ax my grandfather had given me. It was a good honest Swedish ax. Before you could say Jack Robinson I'd felled one of the biggest trees. With a great creak the tree swooshed into the river, and we — the cook, the first mate, me, and three others — were sitting on it, being taken downriver by the current. The Indians stood on the shore, shooting arrows until they were purple in the face, but we were safe, we were. You've got to keep your wits about you, that's what I always say."

Magnus was silent, thinking about what Captain Lillem had told him.

"But you said you were taken prisoner," he said finally. "Did I? Well . . . that's another story, and I think we'll leave that one for another time," said Captain Lillem. "Now we're going to pretend that we want to take Matthew prisoner. We want to steal the money, and we want his motorcycle. After we'd got both these things we'd lock him up. But where? Well, we'd find a place where nobody would be likely to look for him, not in a hurry, anyway, and yet a place he'd

55

manage to escape from in the end. Bad as they are, even thieves and robbers can have a soft heart. Now, where would you lock somebody up if you wanted 'em to be found after an hour or two?"

Magnus racked his brains, but no matter how hard he tried, he couldn't think of a place like that. And, in any case, he didn't know what the houses were like on Ring Island.

"In a factory, perhaps," he suggested.

"Wouldn't take long for him to be found there," said Captain Lillem. "And as for an old shack, well, in one of those he might never be found at all. No, but you see this here old harbor, no depth at all, badly built it was, they're all bandits them that build the harbors these days . . . Now, if they'd only asked me. . . ."

"Do you honestly think that Matthew might be in the old harbor?" interrupted Magnus, "I don't understand."

"Oh no! I s'pose it ain't always easy to follow when us old folks are talking. You see, in that derelict harbor there are some terrible old wrecks of boats; some are lying half-sunk in the water with their backs broken, and some have been lying there ever since I can remember. They are in a pitiful state — all rotten and caved in."

"Goodness! That must be a long time — sixty years! Have you lived down in these parts all that time?"

"Sure! you don't catch me living in the middle of the city — not on your life, you don't — mixed up with a lot of people with nothing better to do than rush hither and thither all day long. They live squashed together in cramped apartments where you can't even keep a dog! Why, life isn't worth living if you haven't got a dog!"

Magnus stopped and gazed at Captain Lillem.

"You mean to say you don't live in the city because you couldn't keep a dog there?" he asked eagerly.

"Of course, I mean it! I live here in a little house I built for Max and me, and there's just enough room for the two of us."

"For Max!" exclaimed Magnus. "Is he your dog, then?"

"Of course! What do you think? He's the best dog in the world."

"I didn't know he was your dog, and I didn't know either that he was called Max, but it seemed the right sort of name for him, so that's what I called him right away when I first met him."

"You're not so dense in the upper story, I can see that. It's not everybody who can take one look at a dog and know his name, but you were quite right."

"I can't keep a dog where I live," said Magnus, "but we're going to move. D'you think I shall be allowed to keep one where we're going to?"

"You never can tell. There's a good chance. Thieves and robbers they are, the whole lot of 'em, but some are soft-hearted all the same, you mark my words!"

The two were now following a narrow path which wound its way down to the harbor. It was a small harbor and it was quite full of wrecks of old boats. There were all sizes of boats there, but none very big and none very small. Nearly immersed in the water was what had once been a respectable barge. To Captain Lillem it was an sad sight, and he heaved a heavy sigh.

"This is where I'd lock up someone that I'd caught," he said at last. "No one comes near this place in the daytime. Only in the evening the down-and-outs come here to sleep, and the lazy sailors who can't be bothered to earn their living, they all come here. Thieves and bandits, that's what they all are, but they would untie Matthew all right and set him free if they found him, that they would. I'm a bit old to be creeping around all these nooks and crannies; you take a look around while I go and put the kettle on for some coffee. Watch your step and don't fall into the water — it's full of rats. You can take Max with you to keep you company."

Magnus nodded.

"You go along with Magnus," said Captain Lillem to Max. "If he falls in the water it's your job to get him out — he's worth saving — must be, or he wouldn't be looking for his big brother as if his life depended on it."

Captain Lillem walked slowly away between two boats which had been dragged up on the shore. Cautiously, Magnus went towards the old wrecks.

58

6

Magnus and Max
Explore the Harbor

THE old steamer looked like the most likely place, even though there were horrid gurgling noises coming from the hold. It looked as though it had a lot of cabins. Magnus was glad to have Max there beside him. His heart was in his throat as he opened one door after another, expecting anything from a rat to a tiger to leap out at him. He could see that Captain Lillem was right; there were signs that people slept here.

Finally they went down into the hold; it was pretty creepy down there, and Magnus was very thankful that he didn't have to live in a place like this. Even having to leave his own cozy kitchen and move to a strange place didn't seem quite so bad now. At least it wouldn't be as ramshackle and frightening as this, and there wouldn't be any wild animals lurking in the corners.

But no matter where they looked, there still wasn't a trace of Matthew. In the end, Magnus went up a ladder and stood on the captain's bridge. Even though he was so anxious about Matthew, he couldn't help thinking what fun it would be to have a really nice ship; to go sailing down the river and to have Father and Mother standing on the quayside, waving to him as he sailed out toward the open sea. Perhaps he would go to South America — not to fight the Indians exactly, but just to take a look at the country. It crossed his mind that Captain Lillem must have been pretty young when he went to South America if he had lived on this island for sixty years since then. Sometimes Magnus imagined lots of exciting things, and he wasn't always so sure if they had actually happened or not — at least, that's how it was when he was younger; perhaps that's how it was with Captain Lillem still.

"Anyway," he thought, "when I'm grown up and have left school, then I'll be a captain, if not before."

Max was standing below on deck, sniffing at the ladder and looking up towards the captain's bridge. He was whimpering.

"All right, fellow!" called Magnus. "You're a clever dog,

but you haven't learned how to climb ladders yet."

When Magnus came down on deck, Max jumped up at him and barked with pleasure. Max couldn't know that Magnus wanted to think about being a captain one day, and that it was a very important matter. Magnus would think more about it some other time when Max wasn't waiting for him.

They went ashore and continued their search on the next ship. It was a barge, but it must have been a long time since it sailed on the river. There was a small wheelhouse on deck and, from this, cabin steps led down into the bowels of the ship. Magnus looked down the steps, but it was pitch black down there, and he couldn't see a thing.

"Matthew!" he called softly. "Matthew! Are you there?"

No one answered. All he could hear was the sound of water swirling around and swishing into the hold, and the noises that came from some cardboard and bits of wood as they floated and bumped against the sides of the ship. There was no sign of Matthew.

Magnus walked around the deck, looking down over the rails to the water below. It was covered with a film of oil; it was black and horrid and dirty. There were bits of timber, scraps of paper, and an old cardboard box floating about on it. Magnus hoped to goodness that he wouldn't fall in; if he did, it would take him weeks to get clean again.

Now there weren't many boats left to look at before they

got to the river, From the next one came sounds of banging and rattling. There must be someone working on it. Magnus decided he wouldn't go aboard; first of all he was a little too shy to go near workmen who were busy on a job. They always seemed to think you got in their way, and if Matthew had been locked up in that boat, the workmen would have found him by now and released him.

So Magnus went to the boat next to it. It had been a nice sailing craft once, but now it was almost completely submerged in the water. It would be quite impossible to hide anybody in that. Beyond it lay a little rowboat, gently rolling on the water, and empty but for a pair of oars.

Magnus was on the verge of tears. He had been quite sure that Captain Lillem was right when he said he thought Matthew must have been locked up in one of the boats down here. Now Magnus had looked everywhere for him and hadn't found him.

Slowly he walked back along the quay. When he came to the boat with the workmen on it he stopped. If he went aboard and was as quiet as a mouse until they looked up from their work, perhaps they wouldn't mind if he asked them if they had seen anything of Matthew. "That couldn't annoy them," he thought, and he had to do *something*. "You've got to get down to things," that's what Father always said. Very quietly Magnus tiptoed aboard.

Max jumped after him, and slowly they walked across the

deck. This, too, was an old barge. It had been called *Else-Marie*. Magnus had seen the name written in large white letters around the stern, and underneath the captain's bridge, too. The sounds of rattling and banging continued, and grew even louder as Magnus went down the steps below deck. The noise was coming from behind a cabin door against which a plank of wood was propped. No doubt the workmen wanted to be left in peace. He was about to walk away, but thought better of it. Creeping softly to the door, he whispered, "Hello! Have you seen . . ."

65

"Magnus!" answered a voice. Magnus nearly fell over in his astonishment and joy.

"Matthew!" he shouted. "What're you doing in there — are you working? Come out, Matthew! I've been looking for you all day, and I've found . . ."

"I can't get out," said Matthew. "The door won't open."

Magnus seized hold of the plank, but it wouldn't budge. In the end he had to bang away at it with a piece of wood. Finally he managed to dislodge it and open the door.

"Easy as pie!" he exclaimed.

"Well, I couldn't manage it," said Matthew, "but then I was on the inside. I suppose that was why."

He gave Magnus a pat on the head, then he went back into the cabin and collected his leather jacket and helmet. He had a black eye, otherwise he seemed to be fine.

"But how did you come to be in there?" asked Magnus. "I've been searching for you all over the place."

"Well, I hadn't much choice," answered Matthew, "but believe me I'm darned glad to see the last of it. I didn't expect to get out of that dump in a hurry. You see, I was attacked by four hefty fellows — one of them went off with my motorcycle, and the other three dragged me along to this boat. They threw me into the cabin, and no matter how hard I tried I just couldn't get out of it. I even broke a table when I was trying to bang down the door, but it wasn't any use. I also tried to get out through the window, but it was much too small. I was about to give up when I heard your voice."

Magnus nodded.

"Didn't you call for help?" he asked.

"Oh no! I think it sounds plain silly when people call for help," said Matthew. "I was sure that one of you — Mr. Lindberg or you — would come looking for me sooner or later."

"Mr. Lindberg! He went ages ago. He gave us two bananas each," said Magnus.

"Oh, grand!" said Matthew. "I wouldn't say 'no' to one at this moment."

"Oh, I'm afraid I gave both of yours to Max. He came, and I was afraid that he'd eat me up, so I gave him the bananas instead, and then he was very good."

"Never mind!" said Matthew quickly. "So this is Max! Nice dog! Hello Max, old boy."

Immediately Max sat down and lifted up his left paw. Matthew bent down and shook it.

"He belongs to Captain Lillem," said Magnus. "Captain Lillem is old, and he's lived here on Ring Island for sixty years. He's been to South America, he says, and to Africa, too, but I think he just thinks he has . . . and I've found your motorcycle!"

"Really!" exclaimed Matthew, amazed. "Where on earth did you find it?"

"Well, first of all I noticed a boy going along on it toward

the city. That made me suspicious. Then I played in the
sandpit with Veronica — she's very nice, she's got a father
who breaks down old cars and a little sister who pours sand
into her hair and shakes it out again."

"That's a strange thing to do!" said Matthew. "You've
met plenty of people, I can see — at least, I suppose you did
meet them — or perhaps you just think you did!"

Magnus felt quite indignant.

"Of course I met them! And they're very nice, too. I'm going to see them again. Veronica can't hear when you talk to her, and she's awfully nice, and she's a bit lonely with no one to play with."

"Good! I mean, I'm glad you're going to see them again, but what happened to my motorcycle?" asked Matthew.

"Well, you see, the fellow came along and propped it against a lamppost. Then I took it and pushed it to the trailer, and Veronica's father hid it in an old bus."

Matthew laughed with pleasure. "You did a splendid job!" he exclaimed. "When I've got a store of my own, I'll make you my manager."

"I'm going to be a captain," said Magnus. "I'm going to sail the sea and look for Africa, and I'm going up a river in South America to see the Indians."

"Right! We'll leave it at that, then. You'll be a captain, and I'll be the first officer, but now I think we'd better make a quick getaway before that gang comes back again."

He led the way up the stairs with Max and Magnus close on his heels. When Matthew came up on deck, he heaved a sigh of relief. Magnus could tell that he hadn't enjoyed being cooped up in that cabin.

"But what about the money?" asked Magnus eagerly as they stood on deck. "What about the hundred and fifty dollars?"

69

"I've got it here," replied Matthew as he pulled an envelope out of his trouser pocket. "The motorcycle seemed to be all they were after . . . or . . . do you think . . . ?"

Matthew stood deep in thought for a while.

"What was that you were going to say?" asked Magnus when Matthew did not finish the sentence.

"Well, I was just thinking — supposing they were just fooling around, perhaps they just locked me in for a laugh?"

"Well, I really don't know what you're talking about — they stole the motorcycle, didn't they?" said Magnus.

He jumped down on to the quay, and Max jumped after him while Matthew stayed behind on deck, still thinking about whether the boys had simply been a bit mischievous.

Suddenly, shouting and calling out to each other, four fellows came running along the road, making for the quay and the old barge. Magnus saw that they were a lot older than Matthew and, among them, he recognized the dark haired boy whom he had seen on Matthew's motorcycle.

"Here's the gang now!" called Matthew to Magnus as he jumped down on to the quay beside him. Magnus stood riveted to the ground with fright. Max, on the other hand, was calmly wagging his tail. He wasn't going to be much use, Magnus could tell that at a glance.

"Here!" breathed Matthew as he pulled the envelope with the money out of his pocket. "Quick! Take this and make a dash for it while I try and keep them busy. Maybe they're

just fooling around — I don't know — they could be up to
no good, though."

Magnus hesitated for a moment, but Matthew gave him a
push. Quickly, Magnus pushed the money inside his shirt
and ran for all he was worth toward the river. He could hear
Max panting beside him. When he turned to look, he could
see that the boys were now quite close to Matthew.

Matthew was still standing in the place where Magnus
had left him, and he was holding a plank of wood in his
hand. Magnus couldn't quite understand how Matthew

could be so brave as to stay behind, all alone, to try to hold off four boys who were so much bigger than himself. But he hadn't time now to stop to think about it. He ran on until he reached the river, but there he couldn't get any further. On one side of him there was a high fence, and straight in front of him was the water. Magnus came to a halt, and now he noticed that two of the boys had run straight past Matthew and were chasing *him*.

Magnus moved a few steps forward, but he couldn't very well swim out into the river. Besides, he wasn't a very good swimmer. Father had said that he really must learn to swim expertly this summer. But the summer had only just begun, and they weren't going to the island until Father started his vacation the end of July.

The boys were getting closer. Suddenly Magnus remembered what Captain Lillem had told him. When the Indians came, he felled a tree, and they all went floating down the river. Magnus didn't have an ax, though, and there wasn't a tree anywhere around as far as he could see. Instead there was the rowboat, and that was a lot better than a tree, really — at least if you were used to rowboats. Magnus wasn't. He had been in a rowboat just once, and then he had been absolutely certain that it would sink, and that they would all end up at the bottom of the lake — but they hadn't.

He had no choice now. He leaped into the boat and lifted the mooring rope which was looped around a post. Quick as

a flash, Max had also taken a jump into the boat. Magnus picked up one of the oars and pushed the boat away from land, just as he had seen Father do, and really it wasn't at all difficult. After only one good shove the boat was already a good distance away from land, and the boys on the shore stopped in astonishment. Magnus put the oar back in its place, because he didn't have any idea how to row. Instead, he sat down very close to Max, hoping that the boat wouldn't float back to the shore.

Luckily it didn't. It floated gently away from the land and then began to be carried down the river by the current. Now Matthew and the other two boys had come running, and all

73

five of them were standing there on the shore, staring after Magnus and Max and the boat.

"Come back, Magnus!" called Matthew frantically.

"Yes, come back, Magnus!" shouted one of the other boys. "We weren't going to hurt you."

Magnus said nothing. The boat was getting further and further away from land; before long it was quite a distance below the old harbor. There were two big black icebreakers moored behind the red fence, and presently the five boys and the old harbor had disappeared behind the icebreakers.

"Get back!" they called again and again, but Magnus sat quite still and didn't answer.

Max, too, sat still. Only the boat moved as it drifted down the slowly-flowing river.

7

On the River

SLOWLY, slowly the boat floated down the river with Magnus and Max. Max sat calmly, taking a good look around, but Magnus was so scared the blood seemed to be turning to ice in his veins. It was a rather small rowboat, and he felt certain that it would tip over at any moment. But there wasn't any wind at all, and the water was perfectly calm with not even the tiniest ripple.

Max sighed heavily and settled himself down on the bottom of the boat. Immediately it rocked dangerously. Magnus caught his breath, but all went well. Now he could feel something pricking inside his shirt. Very slowly, he moved his hand to feel what it was that could be there. It was the envelope. Oh yes! Of course! The envelope with the money. Thank goodness he hadn't dropped it in the water in his haste! Carefully, he brought it out and put it into the pocket at the back of his trousers and did up the zipper.

He didn't feel quite so scared now and he began to look around. The boat drifted slowly along the shore of Ring Island, about a few hundred yards from land. He could see the wooden props which had been driven in along the bank. "The props must be there to stop the shore from being eaten away by the flow of the river," he thought, "and by the big waves that hit it when the ships pass." He watched the reflections of the props on the water, and how the sunshine had faded the paint on them. It was really very nice and peaceful sitting here by himself in a boat of his own, floating along without having to make any effort to do anything.

Now he was gliding past one of the bigger docks which had a groin to protect the entrance. A fishing vessel was anchored there, and a few small craft and a black tug. It was going to be interesting to see the long line of docks on the city side of the river. Magnus knew them all by name, but he had never seen them from the river before. He knew the jetty where all the steamers went from, a big wide stone jetty which sticks out into the river. He knew the fishing harbor with all the vessels that go out into the North Sea and bring back schools of herring and other fish. All the way down

there are big docks, and here, by the city, the river turns gently before it runs out into the sea. On the opposite side of the river, facing Gothenburg, there is a long line of smaller harbors. Those which line Ring Island are quite shallow, and some are connected to small wharfs and factories inland. It was past these little harbors that Magnus and Max were drifting in the rowboat.

The current was now taking it sideways. Ahead of him Magnus saw the great Hising Bridge which spans the river. He hoped he wouldn't collide with one of the high pillars which supported the bridge. Apart from this anxiety he felt quite pleased with his voyage so far. He could have done with something to eat while he sat there, though, and of course it would have been a lot nicer if Matthew had been with him in the boat. They could have talked about the different things they saw from here. "Look at that black barge over there!" Magnus would have said, and: "Gee, what a lot of seagulls!" and: "Look! There's a tug coming, I don't think it's spotted us."

You could sit and chatter to Matthew for any length of time. But Matthew wasn't here with him, so Magnus sat very still and quiet and just watched. He was still gliding along the riverbank close to the row of props. It sure was hot; after a while Magnus took off his shirt. "Poor old Max!" he said. "What a pity you can't take your coat off! It's nice and cool without a shirt."

He bent down to stroke Max, but immediately the boat rocked, and Magnus carefully straightened himself and sat bolt upright — he was almost afraid to breathe. But the boat continued to float softly and quietly as before. Max got up and took a good look around. Then he lay down again with a sigh; by now Magnus was becoming quite used to a bit of rocking the moment either he or Max made the slightest movement, and he didn't mind at all. He began to hum a little tune which he had heard his father sing many a time. It had quite a lot of verses to it, and sometimes he had to start all over again because he couldn't remember all the words right away. But at last he got it right and sang it from beginning to end without having to stop to think.

As soon as he had finished that one, he began on another. It was all about a sailor who loved the ocean waves. It was just the right sort of song for a trip like this, though the sailor liked the roar of the storm and the rush of the waves. Magnus couldn't hear either, and that was just as well. It was much better without storms and waves, because if he kept on and on just floating down the river, eventually the river would take him to the sea. He would go past the Vigna Lighthouse, and soon after that he would be out on the Atlantic Ocean. Well, not tomorrow, or the next day perhaps — it was going to take some time at this rate — but in a week's time he might be on the Atlantic.

Then he thought of Veronica. She would wonder why he didn't come to play in the sandpit, and what could have happened to him. Matthew would wonder too, and Father and Mother would think it very strange that he didn't come back.

Come to think of it, he wasn't at all sure that he would like it very much. He would get awfully hungry, and thirsty, too. Now he rather hoped that he didn't get as far as the Atlantic, and that he would be ashore again before bedtime. It would be very much more comfortable to go to sleep in the alcove off the kitchen than to toss about in the dark on the river all night.

The boat was gliding along past another wharf. He could see three tall trees by the edge of the water. It was very hot now, and there was not a breath of wind to stir the leaves. The sound of cars honking and the roar of an engine revving floated over the still water. Above all there was the squawking of seagulls and from the distant shore the persistent squeaking of a crane. A long train, pulling in alongside the quay, stopped for a minute, and then it drew out again. There must be a lot of traffic in the streets behind the quay, because Magnus could hear the sounds of many cars and motorcycles.

Now a white-painted barge suddenly appeared, coming from up the river. It was going to pass quite close to the little rowboat. What would happen when it was caught in the wash from the big boat? Magnus gripped the edges of his little craft. The white barge came closer and closer. A sailor was standing on it, looking toward Magnus. Suddenly he called, "Hi there! Out fishing?"

At first Magnus was afraid to answer; he wasn't at all used to sitting in a boat, calling out to people in passing barges. But after a while he shouted, "No, I'm not fishing!"

At the sound of voices Max woke and stood up to see what was going on.

"Nice dog you've got there!" called the sailor who was dressed only in a pair of trousers, and whose skin was so brown that, at first sight, Magnus thought he was wearing a brown T-shirt.

"He's called Max," shouted Magnus.

"Max!" repeated the sailor. "Why! My name's Max!"

Magnus had his doubts about that and sat silent.

"But that doesn't prevent him from being a nice dog all the same," called the sailor.

By this time the barge had nearly passed the rowboat. It was far out in the river, about fifty yards away from Magnus.

"You'd better hang on," called the sailor, "there's going to be a big wash from this boat."

"I know there will be," shouted Magnus.

"Of course you do," replied the sailor. "I expect this isn't your first trip down the river."

Then the sailor waved goodby to him, and Magnus stretched himself and waved back. It was really very nice for sailors to hail each other as their boats passed, and he decided then and there that when he became a captain he was going to call out a friendly greeting to every ship he met.

Now came the swell from the barge, but not a very big one, after all. The little boat rocked five or six times and then continued calmly and quietly as before. The barge went on its way toward the Hising Bridge, and was able to pass under it without having to wait for the spans to be lifted.

Magnus's boat was now getting near the bridge, too, and he could already hear the roar of traffic up there. Above all he could hear the clanging of the trams and the singing of their wheels against the rails as he was passing underneath the bridge. He hoped the bridge wouldn't collapse on top of him. When you're *on* the bridge, it seems quite high — from it you can see a long way up and down the river — but when you're underneath, in a little rowboat, it looks like an arch, reaching as high as the sky. The underneath of the arches was patterned with iron beams, and thick metal supports reached down from the bridge into the water. There was a large white notice board on one of the supports which had written on it in big black letters:

MAXIMUM HEIGHT 60 FEET

As Magnus floated past the pillars beneath the bridge, the roar from above became quite deafening, but as he came out on the other side, the sounds gradually grew less.

On the shore he now saw a large building with BANANA COMPANY written on it in huge letters. In front lay a gray vessel with a lot of windows which looked like a Noah's Ark. Magnus had a good look at it as he slowly passed, but he couldn't see anyone moving about on it.

From time to time Magnus looked in the bottom of his little boat to see if it was letting in any water. But evidently it was a good boat because it hadn't let in one single drop. The boat which he and Father had been out in last summer had been so leaky that they had to bail out all the time. Thank goodness he didn't have to do that in this boat!

Soon he would reach the second bridge across the river. It is an old wooden one and not strong enough for any traffic except motorcycles and bicycles. You can walk across it, too, but cars and trucks are not allowed to go over it. It's not nearly so high as Hising Bridge, only a few yards above the water, and instead of having moving spans it works like a drawbridge.

Slowly but surely Magnus approached it. He felt certain the boat would get wedged in the sides of the bridge, because there were long rows of wooden props going down into the water. If Magnus could only hang onto one of them, he might be able to climb up on the bridge. Then he could easily run back underneath Hising Bridge to Ring Island and find Matthew again.

But at the last moment the boat was caught in the current and carried off in mid-channel, more swiftly than before. There was only about a yard between Magnus and the bridge above him, and he stretched up his arm to try to get a hold, but he didn't dare risk standing up for fear the boat might tip over. A moment later he had shot under the bridge and

was on the broadest part of the river. On the city side there was a small harbor where the sailing ship *Viking* was anchored, its gleaming white paintwork glinting in the sun. On the opposite side he could see the enormous Free Harbor with great ships that go to Africa and South America. A little further along he could see another great harbor, and when you are in a little rowboat, all those big harbors and the wide river appear to be like a big lake.

From one of the harbors Magnus heard the sound of a bell, and when he turned his head, he saw the black ferryboat, which plies between one side of the river and the other, emerging. As far as he could see, he and the ferry were bound to meet in the middle of the river. The ferry was big and black and made of iron, so the little rowboat would come off the worst in the encounter and so would Magnus and Max.

At this point Max stood up and watched the approaching ferry with interest. Behind the ferry Magnus could see a cluster of cranes and rusty iron shapes — the great wharf of the Gotha Works. Magnus had hoped to glide near to this wharf, so that he could see everything at close quarters. Now, it seemed that all he was going to see was the ferry, and that at *too* close quarters.

The ferry and the rowboat approached each other, but when they were within fifty or sixty yards, Magnus's boat began to float away, and Magnus heaved a sigh of relief. Max seemed to feel the same way about it. He yawned and settled himself down to sleep again in the bottom of the boat. The ferry sailed past, and now Magnus began to get close to the Gotha Works. The clanking and rattling of welding and drilling resounded across the water, and Magnus could see the bright blue flames in the welding shops. He settled down comfortably. There were some big ships at anchor in front of the works, but Magnus's progress was so slow that he had a good view between the ships as he passed along.

In one place he could see that they had just started building a ship, and the great girders, which were to form the framework of the ship, reared up like enormous ribs. An-

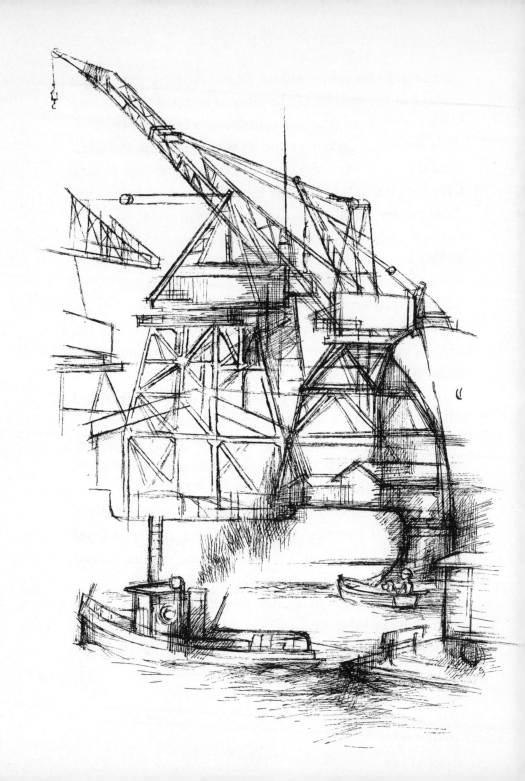

other ship seemed to be nearly completed, but it hadn't been painted yet. It had no rail, and no captain's bridge or anything on the deck. Magnus knew quite a bit about building ships, because his father had often taken him to the stone jetty where the steamers were moored. From there you could look right into the center of the Gotha Works.

Magnus reached the bend in the river, and he lost sight of the Hising Bridge behind the row of ships by the Gotha Works. The rowboat was now floating closer and closer to these ships. They had no cargo and rose so high in the water that they seemed to tower far above Magnus and Max in their little boat. Magnus had to lean right back even to see the rails. This was a busy part of the river; instead of being calm, the water was beginning to be choppy, and the little boat was rocking all the time. But Magnus was getting used to it and it didn't frighten him any more. He hung on to the edges of the boat and was careful not to stand up. Max yawned again and gave Magnus an affectionate glance before he shut his eyes and went to sleep once more.

One steamer after another began to leave the jetty and to sail down the river to its destination in the islands. Two black barges were now coming up the river toward the Hising Bridge, but it seemed that everyone on board was much too busy to notice the rowboat containing Magnus and Max. A large white yacht was being towed up the river by a barge, and there was a hissing sound from the bow as it cut its way through the water, making deep, frothy waves. A rope from its stern linked it to another tugboat which held the yacht steady and in its position on the river and prevented it from swinging into any other boats.

Then Magnus was astounded to see a tug pulling a row of railroad cars. At least, that's what it looked like, but when he looked more closely he discovered that there were three barges with water up to the gunwales, carrying the six cars. A sailing dinghy followed with sails hanging limp, and with an outboard engine chugging in the stern — "Good thing, too," thought Magnus, "with no wind about today."

Magnus was getting very hungry, and by the look of Max, who was sniffing around, the dog seemed to think something was amiss, too. It was an interesting trip all right, but at the present rate of progress they could take a whole week, gliding along quays. Magnus really was beginning to feel that he wanted very much to be on shore again.

Once more they passed a dock, this one full of vessels of all colors and sizes. Then they reached a quay with a notice board saying that this was Lindholmen Wharf. This was a hive of industry, for big ships were being built here among sounds of rattling and swishing and banging. On the opposite side of the river there were no more small vessels, but great Atlantic steamers painted in many colors, and in the middle of the waterway lay ships, moored with great thick ropes to some red buoys.

It wouldn't be long now before they reached Sanna Harbor. Just before they did, they would reach a small promontory below a rock. There were several cottages on that rock, and in one of them lived Mr. Lindberg. Magnus had visited Mr. Lindberg and his wife with Matthew, and he knew that if he could only get close enough to land, that would be a good place for jumping ashore. He looked at the oars. He had a fair idea what to do. Cautiously he lifted them up and dipped them in the water. At first, the boat only splashed from side to side and swiveled around. Then Magnus remembered what his father had done, and he tried to row with long strokes. But there were no rowlocks to secure the oars, so they simply slithered along the gunwales. Magnus very nearly lost them overboard. At one time he felt as if his left arm had jumped out of its socket.

Then he spotted four sticks in the bottom of the boat. He pulled the oars out of the water, put the sticks into the two holes on each side of the gunwales, placed the oars between them, and started to row again. This time he got on very well. Max stood up and was watching these proceedings with great interest.

Magnus looked around him. Soon he found that they were below Lindholmen Wharf. He could see a row of big shiny containers there. He guessed they were full of oil. That was the place where he must try to get ashore; if he couldn't, he didn't know how long he might have to sit in the drifting

boat. Gingerly, he rowed towards the shore, the little boat
making slow and unsteady progress. He saw beneath the
water a sunken rowboat, and then two more boats moored
to a post. He did his best to guide his little craft toward
them. Suddenly he heard someone calling his name, and
when he turned his head, he saw Matthew standing on the
shore together with a lot of boys and girls about the same age
as Magnus.

In his excitement, Magnus let go one of the oars to wave
to his friend. The oar very nearly fell into the water, and
while he was trying to catch hold of it, the boat turned
around and began to drift toward the center of the river.

With renewed effort Magnus managed to turn the boat. Now he was getting close to the shore at last.

"Good work!" shouted Matthew. "Try to get a bit closer, then I can help you."

"Hurrah for Magnus!" shouted one of the boys. "We'll soon pull you in."

"He's awfully clever!" said one of the girls. "I would have died of fright."

Magnus was too preoccupied with preventing the boat from slipping out and being caught up in the current again to pay much attention to what they were saying. At long last he was rewarded by feeling the bottom of the boat scraping the gravel in the shallow water at the edge of the shore.

The next moment Matthew had grabbed hold of the prow and swung the little boat ashore. Max wasted no time in jumping onto dry land. Matthew lifted Magnus out. Magnus stretched himself. It felt strange to be on firm ground again. He had the feeling that he had been sitting in the boat for several hours. Indeed he had! Matthew now told him it had taken him nearly three hours to make his voyage from the old harbor on Ring Island down here to Lindholmen Wharf.

8

A New Neighbor

"I've been keeping an eye on you!" said Matthew. "You know, those fellows who stole the motorcycle only did it for a lark; they didn't really mean any harm. They thought better of locking me up like that and were just coming back to let me out. When they saw that I was already free, they started their bullying games again until they saw you floating off down the river, and then they were really very sorry. The one you saw on the motorcycle was the most upset of all and said he'd jump in the river if anything happened to you.

"I had to say I thought you'd be all right, to calm him down. What a life! I fetched the motorcycle from the yard, but hadn't time to explain to them what had happened. Anyway, Veronica called out to tell you not to forget to come again.

"First of all, I rode to the promontory on Ring Island, but you'd already floated past it, then I waited for a time by the Old Bridge, but couldn't see you, so I went up in Hising Bridge. Then I went back to the Old Bridge, but you were just beyond it. I called out to you, but you didn't hear me. I thought you were going to collide with the ferry. . . ."

"I thought so too, and so did Max. He really looked frightened," said Magnus.

Now he noticed that all the boys and girls were standing in a circle around them, listening, and he felt shy.

"I would have known what to do if I had been in your shoes," said one of the boys.

"Oh. You'd have spent all your time crying, and calling for your Mommy," broke in one of the girls.

"Not on your life, I wouldn't," asserted the boy.

"Is your name Magnus?" asked another of the boys.

Magnus nodded.

"Well, Magnus, why don't you come over to our place to play one of these days? Or you could come out with us to the island? We've got a boat there and I go out fishing with my father. The trouble is, I don't know anyone there, and it would be good fun if you could come."

It crossed Magnus's mind that this boy didn't know him

either, but he didn't say anything. The boys and girls seemed a friendly group, all smiles, and one of them gave Magnus some chocolate. They all knew Mr. Lindberg and his horse, Mary, and you could tell they were both great favorites, but everyone seemed to think that Mary was getting rather old now.

"Well," Matthew went on. "I kept following you along the quay, and I thought that when you got near here, it might occur to you that you could use the oars to row ashore. I thought you might be rather tired, and might feel you had had enough of being a captain for one day."

Magnus laughed. He felt quite pleased with his world at this moment. He only wished that they were moving to *this* place where he now had such a lot of new friends. Then they would be able to climb rocks and talk about boats all the time. But it wasn't here that they were coming; they were moving to a strange new part of the city. Magnus wondered if the children there were just as nice as these. He wasn't so sure about that, but he hoped they were.

"What are you going to do with the boat?" asked a small boy. "Can I have it?"

They all laughed, except Matthew who looked thoughtful and scratched his head.

"Oh yes," he said. "The boat! We can't leave it here; the police might come and say we've stolen it from Ring Island."

"But I didn't steal it," said Magnus. "It just happened that I jumped into it to escape."

"That's no good for an explanation," said Matthew. "We've got to take it back to where it belongs."

They all stood in silence for a long time, thinking hard. Magnus wished that Mr. Lindberg would come and help them think. He always kept calm and knew what to do.

Suddenly Magnus had a bright idea.

"I know!" he said eagerly. "We'll ask Mr. Lindberg to

95

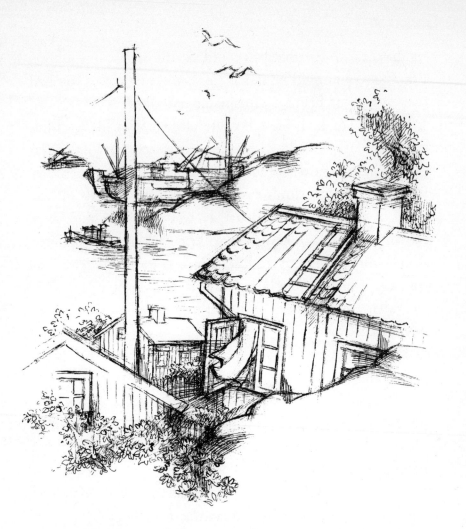

come with Mary and the wagon."

"Good idea!" exclaimed Matthew. "You're full of good ideas today! Of course we can ask Mr. Lindberg. Come along!"

While the children stayed by the boat, Magnus and Matthew walked up to the cottage where Mr. Lindberg lived. The cottage was set high on the edge of the rock, and from it you could see the Vinga Lighthouse far out to sea, as well as the city and the river. It was a wonderful place to live, with the whole harbor stretched out around and below. Magnus hoped that if he couldn't be a sea captain, he would have a cottage like this to live in instead.

They found Mr. and Mrs. Lindberg sitting down to a meal of fried bacon with onion sauce and potatoes. The sight of it made Magnus feel that he would gladly have put up with an even longer voyage if only he had such a dinner waiting for him.

"Well," said Mr. Lindberg, scratching his beard, when he heard what they wanted. "I'm supposed to be going to the Volvo Works . . ."

"But why should you and Magnus want to take the boat up there?" asked Mrs. Lindberg.

"Magnus jumped into the boat, and it floated with him in it right down here," replied Matthew.

"But, Magnus! Is this really true? You'll have to tell us all about it," exclaimed Mrs. Lindberg. "You must be ravenous! My grandfather always used to say that the sea makes you hungry."

Magnus nodded. He felt that Mrs. Lindberg's grandfather was quite right, the sea did make you as hungry as a hunter.

"You've got to tell us all about the trip!" repeated Mrs.

Lindberg as she laid places for Magnus and Matthew at the table.

"Yes," said Matthew. Then he looked at Magnus.

"Well," said Magnus, "I sat in the boat, and it floated down here."

He knew there was a bit more to tell, but at this moment he hadn't a thought but food left in his head. Matthew piled up creamed potatoes and masses of bacon in front of Magnus, and while he was doing so, he told Mr. and Mrs. Lindberg about Magnus's adventure.

To Magnus it had all seemed a bit different from the way Matthew described it, but then Matthew hadn't been in the boat, he had only been on the shore. Nobody could possibly know what it had been like to be in the boat. Anyway, what did it matter? All that mattered now was to be eating bacon with onion sauce and creamed potatoes.

When everyone, even Magnus, had had enough to eat, Mr. Lindberg stood up and said, "If we can manage to heave the boat onto the wagon, it won't be difficult to take it up to Ring Island. Mary is just down below."

So Mr. Lindberg went to fetch Mary, and all the boys and girls wanted to help Matthew and Magnus lift the boat on the wagon; even a little boy called Peter tried to lend a hand. But even though there were more than ten of them, and no matter how much they heaved, the boat wouldn't budge.

"Hey there!" called Mr. Lindberg to a truckdriver and

three other men who were standing nearby. "Could you give us a hand? This boat is as heavy as lead."

"Why, it looks as light as a feather!" exclaimed the truckdriver. "We'll do that easy!"

Mr. Lindberg and the three men gave a colossal heave which brought the boat halfway up onto the wagon, then another great heave, and it was resting securely on top.

Magnus could tell they were strong and used to lifting great weights. They had bulging muscles in their arms. Perhaps it would better to be a truckdriver than a captain. If you had strong muscles, nobody would dare to make trouble with you; all you would have to do would be to bend your arm and show your strong muscles — that would put a stop to their nonsense right away. Even Matthew looked rather slight compared with the truckdriver!

"Where are you taking that old tub?" asked the driver.

"Magnus and Matthew, here, have to get it back to the Old Harbor on Ring Island," answered Mr. Lindberg. "I've promised to give them a hand. Haven't the time, really, but it can't be helped."

"Why didn't you say so right away," said the truckdriver. "I'm just on my way up there with an empty truck. I can take it, if you like — and the boys as well. Won't be any trouble for me at all."

"I'd be much obliged," said Mr. Lindberg.

"Another heave, then!" called the driver to the other men,

99

and the boat was on the ground again.

"Thank you for helping us," said Matthew and waved his hand as Mr. Lindberg drove away with Mary.

Magnus said goodby to Mrs. Lindberg and thanked her again for the lovely dinner. She told him he was very welcome, and that he should come more often.

The truckdriver had brought his truck down to the shore. It had four wheels at the back and two at the front. He pushed some empty boxes to one side and unhinged the sides of the truck.

"Now for some more heaving!" he called.

It was a bit more difficult this time. The truck was higher than the wagon, but in the end they managed to get the boat aboard. Matthew jumped up, and one of the men swung Magnus up as if he'd been as light as a feather. One of the others lifted up Matthew's motorcycle.

There was a roar as the engine started up, and the truck moved slowly away. The boys and girls followed it a little way, shouting and cheering — all of them except Peter who was nowhere to be seen.

Matthew sat down in the boat. Magnus couldn't help laughing.

"First I went in a row boat on the river, and now we're going in a row boat on land!" he exclaimed.

"You're a lucky fellow!" said Matthew.

Magnus hadn't time to answer before they heard a sound

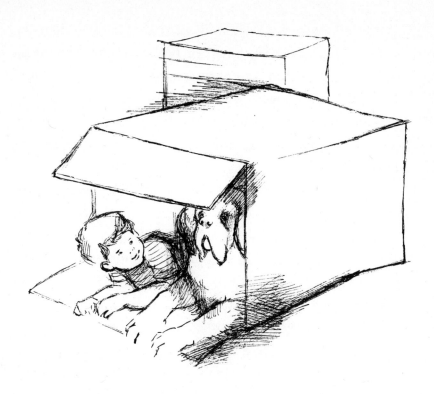

of scratching coming from one of the empty cardboard boxes in front of them and saw Max coming out of it, followed by Peter.

"I've come, too," said Peter. "They lifted me up with the dog. I'm not a bit afraid of dogs, are you?"

Matthew only laughed, but Magnus looked quite thoughtful.

"I can't understand why, but I used to be afraid of Max," he said.

"Were you?" said Peter and sat down close to Magnus. "Well, I was a bit, too, but then he licked my face, and I don't think he would have if he meant to bite me, do you?"

"No, I don't think so," answered Magnus.

"How strange," he thought, "to be sitting in a rowboat on top of a truck, talking to Peter just as easily as if he were Matthew!"

Peter kept chattering away about everything he saw in the street, about what the teacher had said at school, about his father's little car, and about when he last went swimming. He kept on chattering nonstop, and Magnus didn't have to say anything.

"Peter!" exclaimed Matthew suddenly, but he couldn't get a word in edgewise.

"Mommy says I talk a lot because there's nobody to play with where I live; only big boys — and they won't play with me because I'm much younger than them," continued Peter. "It's all new houses around where I live. If only some other children came to live nearby, they could play with me. You know, I've got a marvelous car, but it doesn't work any more, and Daddy says he doesn't think he can mend it."

"All right! All right!" Matthew interrupted the stream of words. "Is that your Daddy driving the truck?"

"My Daddy!" Peter laughed as if it had been the silliest question to ask. "Oh no! My Daddy works at the wharf! I saw him working there once and he said — "

"Peter!" Matthew put in rather reproachfully. "You're just like Magnus was last year — either he said nothing at all, or else he chattered away like a magpie."

"Did I?" Magnus sounded surprised.

"You did too," answered Matthew. "But Peter, what about the truckdriver, d'you know him?"

"No," replied Peter, "I've never seen him before, d'you think he's dangerous?"

Matthew shook his head.

"He's not dangerous at all, but if you don't know him why are you coming with us to Ring Island?"

"Because I like Magnus," answered Peter, "and I like you, too, but you're awfully old."

"That's news to me!" remarked Matthew. "But how are you going to get back from Ring Island?"

For the first time Peter had nothing to say!

"The truck is going straight on into the city," Matthew went on, "and Magnus and I are going with it. Max lives on Ring Island, but what about you? You don't live there, do you?"

"But . . ." said Peter and then he was silent. Magnus thought he was going to start crying.

"Where do you live, Peter?" he asked quietly. "Do you live on Ring Island?"

"No-o," answered Peter, "I live in Bishop's Estate."

"Really?" said Matthew, glancing at Magnus.

But Magnus didn't realize what Matthew was getting at.

"D'you know the name of the street?" asked Matthew.

"Summerweather Street," replied Peter with emphasis.

Magnus thought he was joking, it was such a funny name for a street — a nice one, though, just right for a day like this.

"D'you know the name of the street you're moving to?" Matthew asked Magnus.

"No," answered Magnus.

"Don't you know where you live?" asked Peter, shocked. "Then you must come home with me, because I've got a

couch that you can pull out and make into two beds, and
then we can talk until we go to sleep, and when we wake up
we can go on talking . . ."

"Wait a moment," said Matthew. "Magnus! Don't you
know that you're going to live in Bishop's Estate?"

"No, I didn't," answered Magnus, feeling rather ashamed
of himself.

"Hurrah!" shouted Peter, standing bolt upright, but Magnus pulled him down quickly onto the seat again.

Magnus was enjoying the ride. He liked going in the
wagon with Mr. Lindberg, but this seemed even better fun.

105

He could see how the smaller cars and the motorcycles kept carefully out of the way of the big truck. It was going along at quite a high speed, much faster than Mr. Lindberg's wagon with old Mary pulling in front of it.

The gentle summer breeze became quite a strong wind up here, and the rowboat swayed to and fro as though it were still on the river.

"D'you know the name of the street you're going to live on, Magnus?" asked Matthew.

Magnus couldn't be bothered to answer, he couldn't understand why Matthew had to keep on asking all these silly questions. There were better things to talk about when you were having a lovely ride on a truck than about moving to a place you didn't even want to see.

"You're going to live on Summerweather Street," said Matthew.

"Hurrah! Hurrah!" yelled Peter.

Magnus could hardly believe his ears, but Matthew never told a lie, he knew that. Peter jumped up and down, singing and shouting, and Magnus had quite a job to keep him in the boat.

9

Summerweather Street

It did not take the truck long to make the journey past the Free Harbor to Ring Island, and soon they were on the bumpy road leading to the Old Harbor. Then they found the place where the boat had been moored.

"Good work!" exclaimed Matthew. "It would have taken an hour, at least, for old Mary to have brought us here; we're very grateful."

"Well," said the driver, "it was on my way, no trouble at all."

He lifted Peter and Magnus down. Then he helped Matthew with the motorcycle. Max leaped to the ground by himself. It wasn't difficult to get the rowboat down either. Matthew and the driver gave the boat a push, and soon it was in the water in the exact spot where Magnus had found it. Magnus sighed with relief as he let go of Peter's hand and went up to thank the truckdriver.

"Why! It's nothing," replied the driver as he jumped back into his seat and took off with a great roar.

"The money!" exclaimed Magnus, catching his breath as he suddenly remembered it. It wasn't there any more! It was gone! He pulled his shirt off and shook it. Nothing came out. Goodness! What had happened to it? He felt in his trouser pocket — there it was! Matthew heaved a sigh of relief and wiped his forehead. Magnus quickly handed him the envelope and rushed off to rescue Peter who was sitting in the boat, looking for all the world as if *he* was about to set out for a trip down the river, just as Magnus had done.

"Oh no!" called Matthew warningly. "One trip like that in a day is enough for anyone, I've had just about as much as I can stand."

"Get out of the boat and come back at once," shouted Magnus to Peter.

"I think *you've* got a 'little brother' now," Matthew told Magnus. "Look! It's time we were on our way back to the city."

Peter was watching the two of them very intently.

"You're not going to leave Peter behind, are you Matthew?" asked Magnus anxiously.

"Certainly not," answered Matthew. "I've got a much better idea."

Magnus couldn't think what his idea could be, but Matthew didn't stop to explain; instead he started up the motorcycle. Peter looked anxious.

"Up you go!" called Matthew to Magnus. Magnus let go of Peter's hand and climbed up on his usual seat behind Matthew.

"Come along, Peter!" said Matthew.

Peter moved towards the motorcycle, then Matthew lifted him up an sat him down in front. As they left the Old Harbor behind them, Magnus was still wondering what idea Matthew had had.

First Matthew went to the office where he should have delivered the money long ago. On the way Max disappeared, no doubt he found his way home to Captain Lillem. Magnus and Peter waited silently while Matthew went into the office and explained the delay, then they all continued on the motorcycle to the tram stop by the Free Harbor. Here Matthew lifted Peter down and told Magnus to get off, too. Then he gave Magnus money for their fares, explaining that it wasn't allowed for three people to travel on a motorcycle inside the city boundary.

"Get off at Brunns Park," he told Magnus. "You'll find me waiting for you there."

109

"All right," answered Magnus.

The tram doors shut after them, and Peter and Magnus sat down.

"I like going on the tram," said Peter, "when *you're* there — not on my own."

"Why! Don't you like it on your own? I'm used to it!"
Peter looked at him with respect.

"You're big, that's why you don't mind going alone on them," said Peter.

Magnus didn't think he was big — not compared with Matthew he wasn't. Next to Peter he felt quite big, though.

All the way, Peter kept on chattering. The tram traveled swiftly over the bridge, but Magnus didn't miss looking down into the harbor. He could hardly believe that he had floated down there on the water in a tiny rowboat only a short time ago. It seemed more like a dream now that he thought about it. Mother must be very worried that he hadn't come back home yet. The clock at Queens Market showed three-thirty.

The tram was full of people, and it was quite a crush when it was time to get off. Peter took hold of Magnus's hand, and presently they found themselves in East Hamn Street. It was full of traffic, as usual. There was a zooming, droning noise from the long line of cars and motorcycles — very different from the quiet on Ring Island and in the boat. But Magnus was glad to be back again.

They were just about to cross the street when Matthew caught up with them. He had left the motorcycle in the courtyard, and now he helped them across the street.

In the courtyard Magnus stopped, surprised. A truck was standing there, a fairly small one — only a small truck could get through the low, narrow gateway. When Magnus looked more closely, he spotted Mother's sewing machine, then the blue sofa and the kitchen chairs. Father and two other men were coming down the stairs, carrying cardboard boxes and bookshelves.

"Is it today we're moving?" asked Magnus when his father came down again, this time with the big mirror from the hall.

"Yes, we are," answered his father, "and I was just wondering where you had disappeared to, but Mother said you'd gone with Matthew."

"Yes," said Magnus, "I was with Matthew most of the time, but . . ."

"You might as well leave the rest of the story for the moment," said Matthew. "Wait till this evening."

Magnus nodded. He could see that Father hadn't time to listen to his adventure now.

"Are we really going today?" he asked again.

"Indeed we are," answered his father. "You see, we couldn't get the truck any other time — and who is this little chap you've brought along?"

"He's Peter," answered Magnus.

"Yes, I am," said Peter.

"He lives on Summerweather Street," said Matthew, "but he's strayed rather a long way from home, so perhaps he could go with the first truckload."

"I don't see why not," answered Father.

Now Magnus knew what Matthew had meant when he said he had an idea — he'd worked it out that Peter was going to be taken all the way home — right to his doorstep.

Once you start moving, you find you've got many more things than you ever dreamed you had. Matthew had to go off right away — he had other deliveries to make — but Father and the other two men and Magnus kept on for a whole hour, bringing more and more things down. Still there were a lot of things left in the apartment. Peter sat in a corner of the kitchen and drank orange juice. Mother kept getting things ready and making parcels, but busy though she was, she couldn't help laughing at Peter's running commentary.

"I'm awfully glad that you live on Summerweather Street," she said. "Magnus will have a friend there right away."

"Me too," remarked Peter.

"Oh! Won't it be lovely to have a really easy-to-run apartment in a brand new building!" exclaimed Mother.

"I seem to have heard that remark more than once today!" said Father with a laugh.

"But I *am* pleased!" said Mother. "I don't think I've ever been so happy about moving before — to have a large apartment with plenty of light and somewhere for Magnus to play!"

Magnus was silent, he still wasn't at all sure that he was

going to like it in the new apartment.

At last the first load was ready, and Father and the two men got into the front of the truck. Magnus and Peter climbed in after them and sat on their knees. Magnus felt as if he'd been traveling around in trucks, and boats, and on motorcycles for a week, and still his travels weren't over!

The truck with the furniture piled high and securely fastened, moved cautiously out onto the street, then it traveled through Northtown and out onto the Hising Bridge. It took quite a long time before it finally reached Bishop's Estate.

When they arrived Father said to Magnus, "You'd better

take Peter home at once, his mother must be anxious about him."

Magnus nodded. He took Peter by the hand, and together they went along the street. It was all quite different out here — the houses stood far apart, and in between them were rocks of granite and little clumps of trees. A fresh breeze was blowing in from the sea, and it wasn't stuffy like it was in the city.

Peter knew his way home all right, and when they got there, Magnus followed him up the three flights of stairs. He could see that Peter's mother had been worried.

"Lena came in an hour or two ago, and she told me she'd seen you on a truck," she said.

"Yes, I was," replied Peter, "and Magnus, too."

"Is this Magnus?" said Peter's mother. "Hello! I haven't seen you around here before. Have you just come to live here?"

"Yes, they're just moving in, and I must show Magnus my hut, and the place where I think there's a bird's nest — you know, the one I showed to Daddy last Sunday — and I think we'd better help them to carry everything up, and then . . ."

"All right, Peter, all right!" said his mother. "I'm glad you've found Magnus. Now he can be like a big brother to you, and I shan't have to worry about you disappearing any more."

115

"No, that's right," said Magnus, "I'll look after him."

The two boys went down the stairs again. Magnus felt rather pleased; suddenly he'd become a big brother. That's what Matthew had been to him — but Matthew wasn't going to be around any longer. He was going to his home, and it might be ages before Magnus saw him again. Now he had a little brother to take Matthew's place — a little brother who never stopped talking, and who liked climbing around on the rocks so much that Magnus would have to keep an eye on him, or else he might fall and hurt himself.

"Hurry up! Magnus," called Peter. "Come on! I think this would be a good place for a hut, we could make the door here. They're building over there, and I'm sure they won't mind giving us a few bits of wood."

Magnus couldn't help laughing with pleasure. He was beginning to like it here. It wasn't such a bad idea to move now and then, after all.

"We'd better get started," he said.

"Yes, let's!" agreed Peter. "Just what I thought. It's best to do things at once, that's the fun of it."

"Yes!" replied Magnus, "Father says you shouldn't put off till tomorrow what you can do today."

And as they hurried off together to the building site, Magnus was quite sure that he was going to like it in Summerweather Street.